D0604274

MVFOL

THE NIGHTGOWN OF THE SULLEN MOON

NANCY WILLARD

THE NIGHTGOWN
OF THE SULLEN MOON

ILLUSTRATED BY DAVID McPHAIL

A VOYAGER/HBJ BOOK

HARCOURT BRACE JOVANOVICH, PUBLISHERS

SAN DIEGO NEW YORK LONDON

HBJ

Text copyright © 1983 by Nancy Willard
Illustrations copyright © 1983 by David McPhail
All rights reserved. No part of this publication may be reproduced or
transmitted in any form or by any means, electronic or mechanical, including
photocopy, recording, or any information storage and retrieval system, without
permission in writing from the publisher.
Requests for permission to make copies of any part of the work should be mailed
to: Permissions, Harcourt Brace Jovanovich, Publishers, Orlando, Florida 32887.

Library of Congress Cataloging in Publication Data
Willard, Nancy.
The nightgown of the sullen moon.
Summary: On the billionth birthnight of the full
moon, the moon finally gets what she's really wanted –
a nightgown such as people on earth wear.
(1. Moon – Fiction. 2. Night – Fiction. 3. Clothing
and dress – Fiction) I. McPhail, David M., ill.
II. Title.
PZ7.W6553Ni   1983   (E)   83-8472

ISBN 0-15-332876-2   (Library: 10 different titles)
ISBN 0-15-332903-3   (Single title, 4 copies)
ISBN 0-15-332963-7   (Replacement single copy)

For two close readers,
Marge Willard and Viola Lindbloom
—N.W.

For Anna
—D.M.

The nightgown started it all.

It belonged to Ellen Fitzpatrick, who took the clean laundry off the line for her mother and left her own nightgown, blue flannel and stitched with stars, shining, dancing, on the billionth birthnight of the full moon.

The moon watched the nightgown kick and shine. "Women have danced for me. Men have worshipped me. Poets have praised me. No one has ever given me what I really want," said the moon.

"What do you really want?" said the sun.

"I want a nightgown such as people on earth wear when they sleep under warm featherbeds at night."

"But where will you get a nightgown, dear Moon?"

"The same place they do," said the moon.

And she sank slowly to the tops of the hills
and followed the black road into the valley.

She passed a church,

a laundry, and taverns

and came early in the morning, when the brightness was
off her, to a shop where she had often tracked puddles
of light.

The salesgirl stepped forward. "May I help you?"
"I want a nightgown," said the moon.

The salesgirl brought a nightgown printed with small animals. "It is too small," said the moon.

The salesgirl brought a nightgown printed with big flowers. The moon tried it on. "It is too big! Help!" said the moon.

The salesgirl brought a plain nightgown. The moon tried it on. "It is too pale," said the moon.

The salesgirl brought a black nightgown. The moon tried it on. "It is too dark," said the moon.

Then the salesgirl said, "We have no other nightgowns in the store."

"Not *one*? Not one more nightgown hidden in a drawer at the back of the shop?" said the moon.

"Madame, to please you, I shall look," said the salesgirl.

And there, hidden in a drawer at the back of the shop was one more nightgown, blue flannel and stitched with stars, shining and shimmering on the billionth birthnight of the full moon.

"Shall I gift wrap it?" asked the salesgirl.

"No, thank you, I shall wear it home," said the moon.

Joyfully, the moon sailed outside. She passed taverns and a laundry and a church and followed the black road out of the valley and rose into the sky.

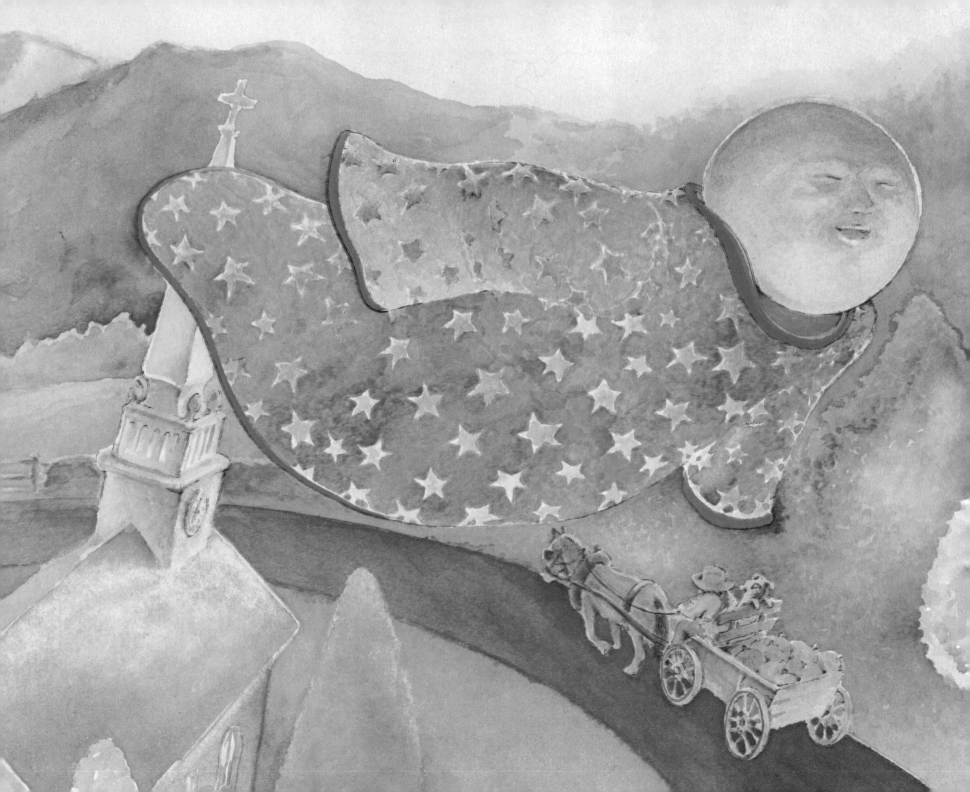

In the evening, people looked for the moon and did not find her.

Men walking on the black road lost their way.

Owls crossing t

ods lost theirs.

Women forgot the words to their songs,

and Ellen Fitzpatrick, waking at night,
saw no dear face in the sky. Outside her
window every singing thing grew still.

And, high and away in her new nightgown, the moon heard people crying for the moon that had left them.

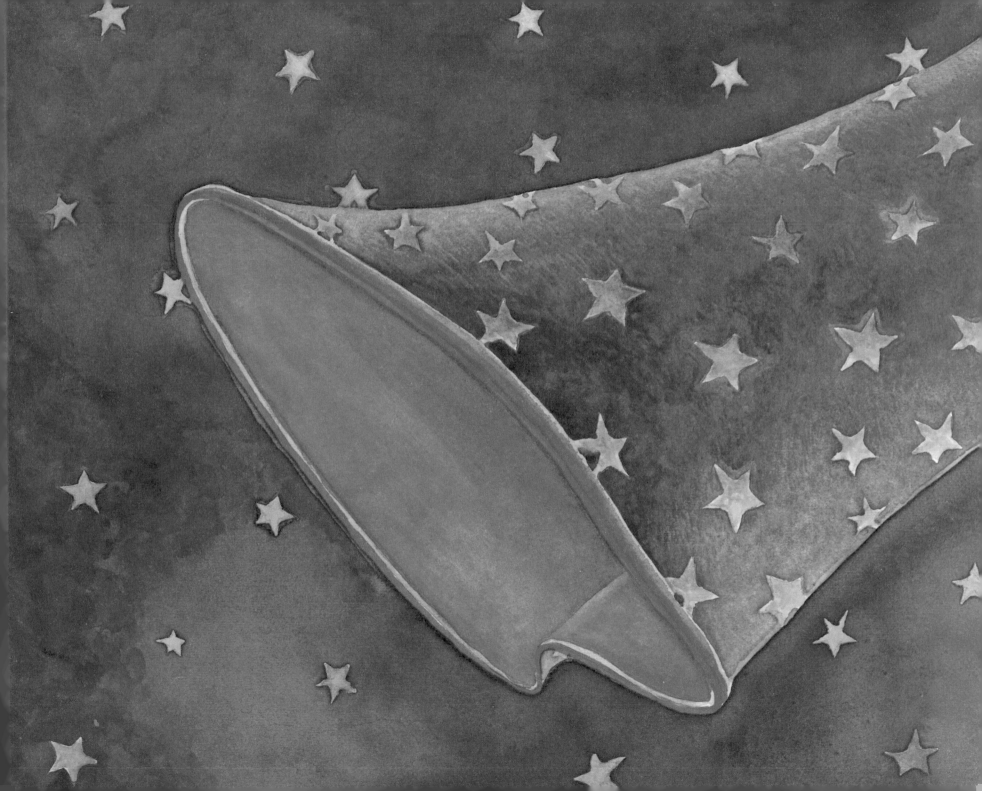

Slowly the moon passed the sun.

"Does no one love my new nightgown?" the moon asked.

"O Moon, people on earth want my gold face in the day and your silver face in the night. So many things change on earth that they want nothing to change in the sky," said the sun. "Take the nightgown back."

"I won't take it back!" cried the moon.

"You must take it back. Promise me you will take it back," said the sun.

"Oh, very well, I promise."

But the moon's promises, what are they worth?
She took the nightgown off, and she hid it in
a drawer at the back of the sky. And on those
nights when you see no moon, you can be sure
she is trying it on and dreaming that she is back
on earth sleeping under the warmest
featherbed in the world.